601

OF THE

FUNNIEST JOKES

AND

ONE LINERS

GUARANTEED TO MAKE YOU LAUGH

JUNE BOURNE

Contents

Be nice to your kids. They'll choose your nursing home.

Children: You spend the first 2 years of their life teaching them to walk and talk.
Then you spend the next 16 years telling them to sit down and shut-up.

Being a great father is like shaving.
No matter how good you shaved today, you have to do it again tomorrow.

My kids have been throwing Scrabble tiles at each other again.
It's all fun and games until someone loses an i.

Before having a kid the most important thing to ask yourself is "Am I ready to watch the exact same cartoon on repeat for the next 4 years?"

The reason grandchildren and grandparents get along so well is because they have a common 'enemy.'

A dad is washing the car with his son. After a moment, the son asks his father, "Do you think we could use a sponge instead?"

My son came home as I was taking his door off its hinges and asked: "Dad what are you doing?" I said, "We've updated our privacy policy."

1 in 5 people in the world are Chinese. There are 5 people in my family, so it must be one of them. It's either my mum or my dad. Or my older brother Colin. Or my younger brother Ho-Cha-Chu. But I think it's Colin.

I childproofed the house... but they still get in!

I never ask my kids to call me, I just change the Netflix password and then don't respond to their texts.

There's nothing I've learned from being a father that I couldn't just as easily have figured out from setting all my money on fire.

That awkward moment when your child looks to you for wisdom and you're like, "Honey, I don't even know what day of the week it is."

I live in constant fear that my kid will become a famous artist or painter and I will have thrown out about a trillion dollars of her work.

My wife gave birth 4 times and still fits in her prom dress from high school. I gave birth 0 times and I don't fit in my pants from March.

My sister bet me I couldn't make a car out of spaghetti. You should of saw her face as I drove pasta.

Money isn't everything but it sure keeps you in touch with your children.

WiFi went down during family dinner tonight. One kid started talking and I didn't know who he was.

My kids are at an age now where they are beginning to understand embarrassment. This is my time to shine.

When I call a family meeting I turn off the house WiFi and wait for them all to come running.

My son asked me what it's like to be married so I told him to leave me alone and when he did I asked him why he was ignoring me.

Women should not have children after 35. Really ... 35 children are enough.

Dad comes to his son and tells him he's adopted. The boy screams "I knew it! I wanna see my real parents!"
Dad replies, "We are your real parents, son. Pack your stuff, they're waiting."

I'll never forget my grandfather's last words to me before he kicked the bucket. He looked me in the eyes and said, "Son, how far do you think I can kick this bucket?"

What did the sick parent make their kids for lunch?
Mac and sneeze!

Child's experience: if a mother is laughing at the father's jokes, it means they have guests.

I tried to explain to my 4-year-old son that it's perfectly normal to accidentally poop your pants, but he's still making fun of me.

My dad died when we couldn't remember his blood type.
As he died, he kept insisting for us to "be positive," but it's hard without him.

Kid: "I'll call you later"
Dad: "Don't call me Later—call me Dad."

Me: "Hey, I was thinking...."
Dad: "I thought I smelled something burning."

People say having kids is the best thing in the world, but you only ever hear that from the victims.

How did the baby tell his mom he had a wet diaper?
He sent her a pee-mail.

Work And Career Jokes

I think that if I died and went straight to hell it would take me at least a week to realize I wasn't at work anymore.

In his job, my dad's never lost a case.
That makes him Gatwick's top baggage handler.

Working at a Hospital is the worst cause you can't call in sick.
You: "Yeah, I can't come in today, I'm sick."
Boss: "Come on in, we'll check you out."

Not to brag, but my antics at work resulted in several items being added to the employee manual.

Ok, what's the latest possible date that I can still make something of my life?

Tomorrow is a big day for me at work.
They are refilling the snack vending machine.

I had a job selling security alarms door to door and I was really good at it.
If no one was home I would just leave a brochure on the kitchen table.

I was once employed by the council to think up new names for all the cul-de-sacs in my town...
It was a real dead end job.

I quit my job at the helium gas factory, I refuse to be talked to in that tone of voice!

Hard work never killed anyone, but why take the chance?

I just got fired from my job as a taxi driver.
Turns out people don't like it when you go the extra mile for them.

I worked in the woods as a lumberjack, but I just couldn't hack it, so they gave me the ax.

I lost my job at the bank on my very first day.
A woman asked me to check her balance, so I pushed her over.

I always put in a full eight hours at work.
Spread out over the course of the week.

I had a job tying sausages together, but I couldn't make ends meet.

Sure boss, I'd love to take on some extra work, I have like 7-8 free hours a night where all I do is sleep anyway.

I didn't know my dad was a construction site thief, but when I got home all the signs were there.

The reward for a job well done is more work.

I used to be a banker, but then I lost interest.

We just got a fax. At work. We didn't know we had a fax machine. The entire department just stared at it. I poked it with a stick.

My job is pretty secure.
No one else wants it.

When my boss asked me who is the stupid one, me or him? I told him everyone knows he doesn't hire stupid people.

My boss is going to fire the employee with the worst posture.
I have a hunch, it might be me.

I just quit my job at a can crushing factory.
It was soda-pressing.

I'm great at multitasking.
I can waste time, be unproductive, and procrastinate all at once.

My boss says I intimidate the other employees, so I just stared at him until he apologized.

I gave up my seat to a blind person in the bus. That is how I lost my job as a bus driver.

My annual performance review says I lack 'passion and intensity.' I guess management hasn't seen me alone with a Big Mac.

I get plenty of exercise – jumping to conclusions, pushing my luck, and dodging deadlines.

How do construction workers party?
They raise the roof.

I'm devastated that my son has chosen a career in finance rather than taking over the family wheat farm.
He's going against the grain.

I like work. It fascinates me.
I sit and look at it for hours.

I don't work well under pressure... or any other circumstance.

I thought I wanted a career, turns out I just wanted paychecks.

My boss just said to me "You've been late five days this week... Do you know what that means?" I certainly do - it's FRIDAY!

I always give 100 %... which is why I lost my job as an exam marker!

A work week is so rough that after Monday and Tuesday, even the calendar says WTF.

Why did the Programmer use the entire bottle of shampoo during one shower?
Because the bottle said "lather, rinse, repeat."

Why do accountants make good lovers?
Because they're really good with figures.

A bus station is where a bus stops. A train station is where a train stops.
On my desk, I have a work station...

When it comes to work, change is inevitable, except from the vending machine.

An archaeologist is someone whose career lies in ruins.

Just saved my boss from a murder.
I went home early.

I came out of the closet to my boss and was fired on the spot.
He's still asking how I got in his closet.
I used to want to become a historian.
Then I realized, there was really no future in it.

My boss asked me to start the presentation with a joke.

So I put my paycheck as the first slide.

I don't always ask my employees how they are.

But when I do, I walk away before they can answer.

If Apple delved into the car manufacturing market, would they have Windows?

I got fired from the orange juice factory...I just couldn't concentrate.

If at first you don't succeed, don't try skydiving.

I heard Cinderella tried out for the basketball team, but she kept running away from the ball.

Why should you never break up with a goalie?
Because he is a keeper.

"I ran a half marathon" sounds so much better than, "I quit halfway through a marathon."

Why is the tennis player such a good lover?
Excellent ball-handling skills.

Why did the soccer player take so long to eat dinner?
Because he thought he couldn't use his hands.

Why is a football stadium always cold?
It has lots of fans!

It takes a lot of balls to golf like me.

I saw a guy spill all his Scrabble letters on the road.
I asked him, "What's the word on the street?"

Why are basketball courts always wet?
Because the players dribble.

Why did the golfer wear two pairs of pants while he played?
In case he got a hole in one.

Why should you never date a tennis player?
Because love means nothing to them.

The triple jump world record is only a hop, skip and a jump away.

Why do bowling pins have such a hard life?
They're always getting knocked down.

What social event do spiders love to attend?
Webbings.

I told my niece that I saw a moose on the way to work this morning.
She said, "How do you know he was on his way to work?"

What's a cow's favorite holiday?
Moo Year's Eve.

Someone asked me how you weigh an elephant.
It's quite like weighing a person, but on a much larger scale.

Why don't you see dinosaurs at Easter?
Because they're eggs-tinct!

What do you call a pig that does karate?
A pork chop.

My obese parrot died.
It was a real weight off of my shoulder.

What do you call a dog who goes to the beach in the summer?
A hot dog.

Why did the elephants get kicked out of the swimming pool?
Because they couldn't keep their trunks up!

What did the Dalmatian say after lunch?
That hit the spot!

What animal is always at a game of cricket?
A bat.

How do you get a squirrel to like you?
Act like a nut.

You think swimming with sharks is expensive?
Swimming with sharks cost me an arm and a leg.

How does a penguin build its house?
Igloos it together.

Why didn't Noah swat those two mosquitoes?

What do you call a cow during an earthquake?
A milkshake.

I named my dog 6 miles so I can tell people that I walk 6 miles every single day.

Why did the lion spit out the clown?
He tasted funny.

What do you call a dinosaur that crashes his car?
Tyrannosaurus Wrecks.

If you need help building an ark, I Noah guy.

How does a pig go to the hospital?
Obviously, in a hambulance.

Why did they stop doing tests at the zoo?
Because it was full of cheetahs!

Where does the sheep get his hair cut?
The baa baa shop!

What kind of reptile does PI work and works in personal finance on the side?
An investigator.

Why don't you ever see giraffes in middle school?
Because they're all in high school.

What kind of shoes do frogs love?
Open-toad!

What did Kermit the frog say at Jim Henson's funeral?
Nothing.

What do you call a duck that gets good grades?
A wise quacker.

What do you call a fish without an eye?
A fsh

Where do most horses live?
In neighhh-borhoods!

Why did the Daddy Rabbit go to the barber?
He had a lot of little hares.

Where do you find a dog with no legs?
Right where you left it.

I took the shell off my racing snail, thinking it would make him run faster. If anything, it made him more sluggish.

I just watched a program about beavers.
It was the best dam program I've ever seen.

What do you call a cow with no legs?
Ground beef.

I threw a ball for my dog... It's a bit extravagant I know, but it was his birthday and he looks great in a dinner jacket.

Never trust a dog to watch your food.

Why do crabs never give to charity?
Because they're shellfish.

What do birds give out on Halloween?
Tweets.

What do you call a couple of chimpanzees sharing an Amazon account?
PRIME-mates.

Why did the teddy bear say no to dessert?
Because she was stuffed.

Why did the chicken cross the playground?
To get to the other slide.

What kind of math do birds love?
Owl-gebra!

Why do ducks have feathers on their tails?
To cover their buttquacks.

A cop just knocked on my door and told me that my dogs were chasing people on bikes. My dogs don't even own bikes...

A Biologist, a Chemist and a Statistician Are Out Hunting.

The biologist shoots at a deer and misses five feet to the left.

The chemist shoots at the same deer and misses five feet to the right.

The statistician yells "We got him"

I'd tell you a chemistry joke but I know I wouldn't get a reaction.

Scientists say the universe is made up of Protons, Neutrons, and Electrons. They forgot to mention Morons.

To the mathematicians who thought of the idea of zero, thanks for nothing!

How does the moon cut his hair?
Eclipse it.

How do we know Saturn was married more than once?
Because she's got a lot of rings!

What did the science book say to the math book?
Wow! You've got problems.

What do you get if you cross a maths teacher and a clock?
Arithma-ticks!

How does a scientist freshen her breath?
With experi-mints.

Did you hear about the claustrophobic astronaut?
He needed a little space.

I'm reading a book on anti-gravity.
I can't put it down.

Which planet loves to sing?
Nep-tune!

How do you stop an astronaut's baby from crying?
You rocket.

Have you heard about the sick chemist?
If you can't helium, and you can't curium, you'll probably have to barium.

Why can't you trust atoms?
They make up everything.

Parallel lines have so much in common.
It's a shame they'll never meet.

Why is beer never served at a maths party?
Because you can't drive and derive.

What did the math teacher write on his party invitations?
Be there or B^2.

How does NASA organize a party?
They planet.

What did one math book say to the other?
"I've got so many problems."

Why did the peanut get into a rocket?
He wanted to be an astro-nut!

A Wife Sends Her Software Engineer husband to the store.

"Could you please go shopping for me and buy one carton of milk. And if they have eggs, get six!"

Later, the husband comes back with six cartons of milk. The wife asks him why he bought six cartons of milk and he replied, "they had eggs."

My wife is really mad at the fact that I have no sense of direction.
So I packed up my stuff and right!

My buddy set me up on a blind date & said, "Heads up, she's expecting a baby."
Felt like an idiot sitting in the bar wearing just a diaper.

They keep saying the right person will come along, I think mine got hit by a truck.

A man on a date wonders if he'll get lucky.
A woman already knows.

Any married man should forget his mistakes, there's no use in two people remembering the same thing.

I had my credit card stolen the other day but I didn't bother to report it because the thief spends less than my wife.

My wife is on a tropical fruit diet, the house is full of the stuff!
It's enough to make a mango crazy.

Every time you talk to your wife, your mind should remember that...
'This conversation will be recorded for Training and Quality purposes.'

My girlfriend isn't talking to me. She said I ruined her birthday.
I'm not sure how. I didn't even know it was her birthday.

Relationships are a lot like algebra.
Have you ever looked at your X and wondered Y?

The difference between 'Girlfriend' and 'Girl Friend' is that little space in between we call the "Friend Zone."

My girlfriend told me she was leaving me because I keep pretending to be a Transformer. I said, "No, wait! I can change."

Never laugh at your girlfriend's choices... you're one of them.

Adam's girlfriend, Ruth, fell off the back of his motorcycle.
He just rode on. Ruthless.

Losing a wife can be very tough.
Some may even say impossible.

My wife was furious at me for kicking dropped ice cubes under the refrigerator.
But now it's just water under the fridge.

This girl on Tinder asked me why I have an unlit cigarette in my picture...
I told her I'm just looking for matches.

My wife asked me earlier: "Are you even listening to me?"
Which is a really weird way to start a conversation...

My wife is so negative. I remembered the car seat, the stroller, AND the diaper bag.
Yet all she can talk about is how I forgot the baby.

My girlfriend was complaining last night that I never listen to her.
Or something like that...

My wife just found out I replaced our bed with a trampoline; she hit the roof.

A female magician made her boyfriend vanish.
How? By asking for a commitment.

I'm in a long distance relationship.
My girlfriend is in the future.

Two antennas met on a roof, fell in love and got married.
The ceremony wasn't much, but the reception was excellent.

What did the volcano say to his wife?
I lava you so much.

A doctor tells a woman she can no longer touch anything alcoholic.
So she gets a divorce.

Last night me and my girlfriend watched three DVDs back to back.
Luckily I was the one facing the telly.

What did one boat say to the other boat?
Are you interested in a little row-mance?

On a scale of North Korea to America, how free are you tonight?

What do you call a romantic Potato?
A cheesy potato!

I'm no photographer, but I can picture us together.

What did the patient with the broken leg say to their doctor?
Hey doc, I have a crutch on you.

When does a vampire know they're in love?
It's always love at first bite.

Why shouldn't you fall in love with a pastry chef?
He'll dessert you.

What's the difference between love and marriage?
Love is blind. Marriage is an eye-opener.

I asked my wife what she wanted for Christmas. She told me
"Nothing would make me happier than a diamond necklace."
So I bought her nothing.

My girlfriend said, "You act like a detective too much. I want to split
up." "Good idea," I replied. "We can cover more ground that way."

I accidentally handed my wife a glue stick instead of a chapstick. She
still isn't talking to me.

My girlfriend left me because she couldn't handle my OCD.
I told her to close the door five times on her way out.

Time waits for no man, time is obviously a woman.

I like older men because they've gotten used to life's disappointments. Which means they're ready for me.

My husband is on the roof - only a few inches away from an insurance claim that could completely change my life.

To be happy with a man, you must understand him a lot and love him a little.
To be happy with a woman, you must love her a lot and not try to understand her at all.

When a woman says "what?" it's not because she didn't hear you. She's just giving you a chance to change what you said.

I asked my wife if she ever fantasizes about me.
She said yes - about me taking out the trash, mowing the lawn, and doing the dishes.

I married my wife for her looks, but not the ones she's giving me lately.

I seem to have lost my phone number. Can I have yours?

Girlfriend: "Knock, knock."
Boyfriend: "Who's there?"
Girlfriend: "Olive."
Boyfriend: "Olive, who?"
Girlfriend: "Olive you, and I don't care who knows it"

Are you French?
Because Eiffel for you.

You know what I did before I married?
Anything I wanted to.

Most men know that women dream of having two men at the same time. But they don't understand that in those fantasies one man is cleaning the house and the other one is cooking.

What's the difference between a new husband and a new dog?
After a year, the dog is still excited to see you.

My wife had me take out more life insurance and now there's no grip left on the bath mat.
Weird.

I used to date a girl that reported the weather.
We had a very stormy relationship.

I broke up with my girlfriend at a restaurant. She started crying.
Everyone thought I proposed to her so they started clapping.

Coffee, Chocolate, Men. Some things are just better rich.

Sure, I may not be in a relationship, but I am three people's plan B and someone's maybe if we're ever the last two people on Earth.

What's the best part about Valentine's Day?
The day after when all the chocolate goes on sale.

The ideal man doesn't smoke, doesn't drink, doesn't do drugs,
doesn't swear, doesn't get angry, doesn't exist.

Let's commit the perfect crime together.
I'll steal your heart and you can steal mine.

A husband and wife are drinking wine at home
Wife: "I love you"
Husband: "Is that you or the wine talking?"
Wife: "It's me talking to the wine"

We're not socks.
But I think we'd make a great pair.

You are like dandruff.
I just cannot get you out of my head no matter how hard I try.

Why do men like to fall in love at first sight?
Because doing so saves them a lot of money.

Me: "Would you like to be the sun in my life?"
Her: "Awww... Yes!!!"
Me: "Good then stay 92.96 million miles away from me"

My wife and I were happy for twenty years.
Then we met.

Can a woman make her husband a millionaire?
Of course, if he's a billionaire.

Marriage is like going to a restaurant.
You order what you want, then when you see what the other person has, you wish you had ordered that.

Me and my partner were going to go on holiday to Norway this year, but we costed it up and in the end we couldn't af-fjord it.

My wife accused me of being immature.
I told her to get out of my fort.

I'm seriously thinking about re-marrying my ex-wife, but I'm pretty sure she'll figure out I'm just after my money.

I'm single by choice.
Unfortunately, it's not my choice.

The best way to remember your wife's birthday is to forget it once.

My new girlfriend works at the Zoo.
I think she is a keeper.

I love being married.
It's so great to find that one special person you want to annoy for the rest of your life.

It was an emotional wedding.
Even the cake was in tiers.

I think I married someone else's soulmate.
I wish they'd come get him.

I told my girlfriend she drew her eyebrows too high.
She seemed surprised.

A furniture store keeps calling me.
All I wanted was a one nightstand.

A plane crashed in the jungle and every single person died. Who survived?
Married couples.

If you're not supposed to eat at night, why is there a light bulb in the refrigerator?

I didn't fight my way to the top of the food chain to be a vegetarian.

Turning vegan is a big missed steak.

A ham sandwich walks into a bar and orders a beer.
The bartender says, "I'm sorry, we don't serve food here."

I recently added squats to my workouts by moving the beer into the bottom shelf of the fridge.

I thought the dryer was shrinking my clothes.
Turns out it was the refrigerator all along.

When two vegans get in an argument, is it still called a beef?

What did Baby Corn say to Mama Corn?
"Where's Pop Corn?"

I once had a dream I was floating in an ocean of orange soda.
It was more of a fanta sea.

What kind of car does an egg drive?
A yolkswagen.

Whenever I try to eat healthy, a chocolate bar looks at me and
Snickers.

I relish the fact that you've mustard the strength to ketchup to me.

I knew a guy who was going to open a pastry shop.
But he couldn't raise the dough.

What does garlic do when it gets hot?
It takes its cloves off.

Why don't eggs tell jokes?
They'd crack each other up.

What happened when the strawberry tried to cross the road?
There was a traffic jam.

Why did the banana go to the hospital?
Because it wasn't peeling well.

I'm on a seafood diet.
Every time I see food, I eat it.

After an explosion at a French cheese factory... all that was left was De Brie.

Just burned 2,000 calories.
That's the last time I leave brownies in the oven while I nap.

Did you hear about the guy who got hit in the head with a can of soda?
He was lucky it was a soft drink.

How did the egg get up the mountain?
It scrambled up.

Why did the onion need help?
It was in a pickle.

Knowledge is knowing a tomato is a fruit.
Wisdom is not putting it in a fruit salad.

Where do hamburgers go to dance?
The meat-ball.

How do we make an egg laugh?
Tell them a yolk (joke).

How do you make a hot dog stand?
Steal its chair.

The next time you have company, serve them a bowl of shelled peanuts.
After they've eaten a few handfuls, casually mention that you've never liked peanuts, but you love to suck the chocolate off of them.

Fridges should have glass doors.
That way I don't have to stand with the fridge door open trying to figure out my next move.

I need to stop drinking so much milk.
It's an udder disgrace.

How do squids get to school?
They take an octobus.

Why did the donut go to the dentist?
To get a filling.

What did the grape do when he got stepped on?
He let out a little wine.

Hear about the new restaurant called 'Karma?'
There's no menu, you only get what you deserve.

I regret rubbing ketchup in my eyes, but that's Heinz sight.

What kind of nut doesn't like money?
Cash ew.

Why did the tomato blush?
Because it saw the salad dressing.

Planning meals in advance, now that's some food forethought.

Why did the orange stop?
It ran out of juice!

What do ghosts serve for dessert?
I Scream.

What do you call cheese that isn't yours?
Nacho cheese.

What do you call two bananas on the floor?
Slippers.

How do you make a lemon drop?
Let it fall from the tree.

I thought about going on an all-almond diet.
But that's just nuts!

Did you hear about the restaurant on the moon?
Great food, no atmosphere.

What did the guest say when he arrived at the peanut butter's dinner party?
"Nice spread!"

Why did the cookie go to the hospital?
Because it was feeling a little crummy.

Why are pizza jokes the worst?
They're too cheesy.

What fruit do twins love?
Pears!

Why was the baby strawberry crying?
Because their parents were in a jam.

Two monkeys were getting into the bath. One said: "Oo, oo, aah."
The other replied: "Put some cold in then."

What do you call a dog that does magic tricks?
A labracadabrador.

Once my dog ate all the Scrabble tiles.
For days he kept leaving little messages around the house.

Why did the Mushroom get invited to so many parties?
He was a fungi.

What about the shrimp that went to the prawn cocktail party?
He pulled a mussel.

What kind of pictures do turtles take?
Shell-fies.

I saw this bloke chatting-up a cheetah. I thought, "he's trying to pull a fast one."

What's orange and sounds like a parrot?
A carrot.

What do you call a parade of rabbits hopping backwards?
A receding hare-line.

Why can't you trust zookeepers?
They love cheetahs.

What is the smartest insect?
A spelling bee!

What is a cat's favorite dessert?
A bowl full of mice-cream.

How does a clam celebrate his birthday?
It shellebrates!

At a birthday party, how can you tell if a donut is bored?
It looks glazed over.

Why is ice cream always invited to parties?
It's cool.

My friend asked me to help him round up his 37 sheep.
I said "40."

What do you call a bear with no teeth?
A gummy bear!

How was the fish's birthday party?
It went swimmingly.

Who eats snails?
People who don't like fast food!

Why did the student eat his homework?
Because the teacher told him it was a piece of cake.

My math teacher called me average.
How mean!

A teacher asks a student, "Are you ignorant or just apathetic?"
The kid answers, "I don't know and I don't care."

Math Teacher: "If I have 5 bottles in one hand and 6 in the other hand, what do I have?"
Student: "A drinking problem."

Behind every successful student, there is a deactivated Facebook account.

Why did the blue lily get in trouble at school?
For tweeting on a test!

What is a witch's favorite subject in school?
Spelling.

What did the calculator say to the maths student?
You can count on me.

Why did the music teacher need a ladder?
To reach the high notes.

Why did the teacher put on sunglasses?
Because their students were so bright!

Why did the M&M go to school?
Because she wanted to be a Smartie.

Why was the broom late to school?
It over-swept!

What did the elf learn in school?
The elf-abet.

I failed math so many times at school,
I can't even count.

What do farmers do at parties?

They turnip the beets.

I've never enjoyed my surprise birthday parties because all I can think about is how good my friends are at lying to my face.

At a party, a young wife admonished her husband, "That's the fourth time you've gone back for ice cream and cake. Doesn't it embarrass you?"

"Why should it?" answered her spouse. "I keep telling them it's for you."

A boy went to a costume party with a girl on his back. Someone asked his what he was supposed to be. He answered, "a turtle."

"Then why do you have a girl on your back?" the guy asked again.
The boy answered, " it's Michelle."

What did the cannibal get when he showed up to the party late?
A cold shoulder.

What did the tree wear to the pool party?
Swimming trunks.

Why was the birthday boy's party so bad?
Because he was turning farty!

Why did the birthday girl feel so warm at her birthday celebration?
People kept toasting her!

How do you know there is a firefighter at the party?
He's got all the hose.

Why was soap given to the little girl for her birthday?
It was a soap-rise party!

Did you hear about the tree's birthday party?
Things got pretty sappy!

I wonder why the knot wasn't invited to the party?
It was all tied up.

What will you do if no one turns up to your birthday party?
You'll have your cake and eat it, too.

During lockdown: The buttons of my jeans have started social distancing from each other.

I'll tell you a coronavirus joke now, but you'll have to wait two weeks to see if you got it!

So many coronavirus jokes out there, it's a pundemic!

Before lockdown I was lazy.
During lockdown I became lazy max pro ultimate.

During lockdown: "Yeah, I have plans tonight. I'll probably hit the living room around 8 or 9!"

2020 was a Unique leap year. It had 29 days in February, 300 days in March and 5 days in April.

Why did the chicken cross the road?
Because the chicken behind it didn't know how to socially distance properly!

Sleep, eat, repeat.
Regards 2020.

It might take a village to raise a child, but I swear it's gonna take a vineyard to homeschool one.

Remember laughing at Michael Jackson for wearing a mask and gloves?
Now you are all out there looking like you wanna be starting something.

If corona virus isn't about beer, why do I keep seeing cases of it?

I overslept this morning and was late getting to the living room!

Why didn't the sick guy get the joke?
It flu over his head!

Back in my day the only time we started panic buying was when the bartender yelled "Last Call."

Did you hear the joke about covid-19?
Never mind, I don't want to spread it around!

I wish corona could've started in Las Vegas because "What happens in Las Vegas stay in Vegas."

Ordering pizza in lockdown be like: "Leave it on the doorstep and get the hell outta here!"

I swear my fridge just said: "What the hell do you want now!"

The lockdown turned us all into dogs.
We roamed the house looking for food, we were told no if we get too close to strangers and we got really excited about car rides and walks.

My husband purchased a world map and then gave me a dart and said: "Throw this and wherever it lands – that's where I'm taking you when this pandemic ends." Turns out, we're spending two weeks behind the fridge!

Anybody else feels like they cooked dinner about 6,187 times during lockdown?

You sound reasonable. It must be time to up my medication!

What kind of exercise do lazy people do? Diddly-squats.

Dr.'s are saying not to worry about the bird flu because it's tweetable.

Refusing to go to the gym counts as resistance training, right?

Doing things that you are not supposed to do at work makes your vision, hearing and alertness much better.

Why is it everything I love is either unhealthy, addictive or has multiple restraining orders against me?

Last week my Doctor told me I was going deaf.
I haven't heard from him since.

Sometimes I go into the fitting room with jeans three sizes too big so I can feel what it's like to succeed at a diet.

A recent study has found that women who carry a little extra weight live longer than the men who mention it.

My doctor told me that jogging could add years to my life.
He was right—I feel ten years older already.

I always feel better when my doctor says something is normal for my age but then think dying will also be normal for my age at some point.

"Doctor, there's a patient on line 1 that says he's invisible."
"Well, tell him I can't see him right now."

What time is it when you have to go to the dentist?
Tooth hurty!

How do you prevent a summer cold?
Catch it in the winter.

What do you give a sick lemon?
Lemon-aid.

A man tells his doctor, "Help me. I'm addicted to Twitter!"
The doctor replies, "Sorry, I'm not following you."

How do you find Will Smith in a snowstorm?
Look for the fresh prints.

A thief broke into the police headquarters during the night and took all the toilets.
Cops say they have nothing to go on.

Bob The Builder has emigrated and set up a new business on a French Mediterranean island... Can he fix it? Corsican!

What's the best thing about living in Switzerland?
I don't know, but the flag's a big plus.

I was wondering, why does a Frisbee appear larger the closer it gets?
Then, it hit me.

What do you call a boomerang that doesn't come back?
A stick.

What Did E.T.'s mother say to him when he got home?
"Where on earth have you been?"

Did you hear about the guy who invented Life Savers?
They say he made a mint!

How do you make holy water?
You boil the hell out of it.

I'm reading a book on the history of glue.
I can't put it down!

How do you make a Kleenex dance?
Put a little boogie in it.

Did you hear about the kidnapping at school?
It's fine, he woke up.

I don't buy anything with Velcro.
It's a total rip-off.

Why don't skeletons ever go trick or treating?
Because they have nobody to go with.

I needed a password that was eight characters long.
So I picked Snow White and the seven dwarfs.

I once farted on an elevator.
I was rude on so many levels.

What does a storm cloud wear under his raincoat?
Thunderwear.

How does the ocean say hi?
It waves!

Name the kind of tree you can hold in your hand?
A palm tree!

How does a vampire start a letter?
"Tomb it may concern..."

Why can't you ever tell a joke around glass?
It could crack up.

What do you call a Star Wars droid that takes the long way around?
R2 detour.

How do you know when a bike is thinking?
You can see their wheels turning.

Why was 6 afraid of 7?
Because 7,8,9.

How do billboards talk?
Sign language.

What kind of water cannot freeze?
Hot water.

Why was the belt arrested?
Because it was holding up some pants.

Did you hear the joke about the roof?
Never mind, it would go over your head.

How do bees brush their hair?
With honeycombs!

What do you do if someone rolls their eyes at you?
Roll them right back.

What did the bathtub say to the toilet?
"You look flushed!"

How much does it cost a pirate to get his ears pierced?
A buck an ear.

What is a computer's favorite snack?
Computer chips.

How does Spiderman do research?
On the World Wide Web!

What is fast, loud and crunchy?
A rocket chip.

What has ears but cannot hear?
A cornfield.

I threw a boomerang a few years ago.
I now live in constant fear.

Someone stole my mood ring.
I don't know how I feel about that.

How many Germans does it take to screw in a lightbulb?
One – they're very efficient and not very funny.

I broke my finger last week.
On the other hand, I'm okay.

A Roman legionnaire walks into a bar, holds up two fingers and says "five beers, please."

Someone stole my Microsoft Office and they're gonna pay.
You have my word!

I tried to catch fog yesterday.
Mist!

How does Moses make his coffee?
Hebrews it!

I entered ten puns in a pun contest hoping one would win, but no pun in ten did.

The best time to add insult to injury is when you're signing somebody's cast.

I went to buy some camouflage trousers the other day, but I couldn't find any.

Somebody actually complimented me on my driving today.
They left a little note, saying "Parking Fine."

Did you hear about the actor who fell through the floorboards?
He was just going through a stage.

A soldier survived mustard gas in battle, and then pepper spray by the police.
He's now a seasoned veteran.

I was playing chess with my friend and he said, "Let's make this interesting."
So we stopped playing chess.

Why do we tell actors to "break a leg?"
Because every play has a cast.

My grandfather invented the cold air balloon.
It never really took off.

The pollen count, now that's a difficult job.
Especially if you've got hay fever.

Uncle Ben has died.
No more Mr Rice Guy.

I'm addicted to brake fluid, but I can stop whenever I want.

How do you keep an idiot in suspense?

Have you heard about those new corduroy pillows?
They're making headlines.

Exit signs? They're on the way out!

Exaggerations went up by a million percent last year.

They all laughed when I said I wanted to be a comedian.
Well, they're not laughing now.

What does Charles Dickens keep in his spice rack?
The best of thymes, the worst of thymes.

Hard to tell if people are interested in joining my Sarcastic Club or not.

What did the bald man exclaim when he received a comb for a present?
"Thanks! I'll never part with it!"

Why does Snoop Dogg carry an umbrella?
Fo' drizzle

I'm pleased to be getting a beer belly.
I've always wanted a father figure.

I tell my friends I'm here for them 24/7 because it sounds better than saying I'm only here for them on 24 July.

I have a fear of speed bumps.
But I am slowly getting over it.

Have you ever tried eating a clock?
It's really time-consuming, especially if you go for seconds.

Why doesn't the sun go to college?
Because it has a million degrees!

How do trees get online?
They just log on!

What did 0 say to 8?
Nice belt!

I love pressing F5.
It is so refreshing.

A book fell on my head the other day in my office.
I've only got my shelf to blame.

What is the best way to avoid touching your face?
A glass of wine in each hand!

I would never have believed that a few weeks of uncut hair would weigh 20 pounds but that's what the scale says.

Where do sick boats go to get healthy?
The dock!

Ran out of toilet paper and started using lettuce leaves.
Today was just the tip of the iceberg, tomorrow *romaines* to be seen!

Can a kangaroo jump higher than the Empire State Building?
Of course! Buildings can't jump!

What day of the week are most twins born?
Twos-day!

How does a train eat?
It goes chew chew.

Why was the sand wet?
Because the sea weed.

Why couldn't Dracula's wife fall asleep?
Because of his coffin!

Why did the traffic light say to the car?
"Hey! Don't look, I'm about to change."

Why did the skeleton go to the restaurant?
For spare ribs.

Why did the boy sprinkle sugar on his pillow?
He wanted to have sweet dreams.

What do you call a rich elf?
Welfy.

What kind of music scares balloons?
Pop Music!

What are the strongest days of the week?
Saturday and Sunday. All the others are weekdays.

Thanks for explaining the word 'many' to me — it means a lot.

Two burglars stole a calendar last night and they each got six
months.

I just found out I'm colorblind.
The diagnosis came completely out of the purple.

I've just been fired from the clock making factory after all those extra hours I put in.

Why was the man fired from a calendar factory?
He took a day off.

Did you hear about the fire in the shoe factory?
Many soles were lost.

If every day is a gift, I'd like a receipt for Monday.
I want to exchange it for another Friday.

If it wasn't for the last minute, nothing would get done.

I didn't say it was your fault, I said I was blaming you.

He who smiles in a crisis has found someone to blame.

Some mistakes are too much fun to only make once.

Keep the dream alive; hit the snooze button.

I have all the money I'll ever need – if I die by 4:00 p.m. today.

The trouble with being punctual is that nobody's there to appreciate it.

I got carded at a liquor store, and my Blockbuster card accidentally
fell out.
The cashier said "never mind."

I don't trust those trees.
They seem kind of shady.

I don't trust stairs.
They're always up to something.

I used to be addicted to soap, but I'm clean now.

What country's capital is growing the fastest?
Ireland. Every day it's Dublin.

Mountains aren't just funny.
They're hill areas.

Can February March?
No, but April May!

What did one wall say to the other?
"I'll meet you at the corner."

Today a man knocked on my door and asked for a small donation
towards the local swimming pool.
I gave him a glass of water.

I got a new pair of gloves today, but they're both 'lefts' which, on the one hand, is great, but on the other, it's just not right.

I changed my password to 'incorrect.'
So whenever I forget what it is, the computer will say "Your password is incorrect."

I think my neighbor is stalking me as she's been googling my name on her computer.
I saw it through my telescope last night.

Feeling pretty proud of myself. The Sesame Street puzzle I bought said 3-5 years, but I finished it in 18 months.

That awkward moment when you leave a store without buying anything and all you can think is 'act natural, you're innocent.'

I was addicted to the hokey pokey... but thankfully, I turned myself around.

About a month before he died, my uncle had his back covered in lard.
After that, he went down hill fast.

Before I criticize a man, I like to walk a mile in his shoes.
That way, when I do criticize him, I'm a mile away and I have his shoes.

You know you're ugly when it comes to a group picture and they hand you the camera.

A man walks into a bar with a roll of tarmac under his arm and says: "Pint please, and one for the road."

A diplomat is a man who always remembers a woman's birthday but never remembers her age.

Claustrophobic people are more productive thinking out of the box.

I'm not saying your perfume is too strong.
I'm just saying the canary was alive before you got here.

I bought some shoes from a drug dealer. I don't know what he laced them with, but I've been tripping all day.

The older I get, the earlier it gets late.

What's the difference between men and pigs?
Pigs don't turn into men when they drink.

If you think nobody cares whether you're alive, try missing a couple of payments.

I can totally keep secrets. It's the people I tell them to that can't.

I like having conversations with kids. Grownups never ask me what my third favorite reptile is.

Money talks ...but all mine ever says is good-bye.

Thieves had broken into my house and stolen everything except my soap, shower gel, towels and deodorant. Dirty Bastards.

The Man Who Created Autocorrect Has Died.
Restaurant In Peace.

Is your ass jealous of the amount of shit that just came out of your mouth?

Light travels faster than sound.
This is why some people appear bright until you hear them speak.

Whatever you do always give 100%.
Unless you are donating blood.

There are three kinds of people: Those who can count and those who can't.

One day you're the best thing since sliced bread.
The next, you're toast.

People are making end of the world jokes.
Like there is no tomorrow.

Eat right. Stay fit. Die anyway.

Let me make this simple, I want to be invited but I don't want to go.

Police have arrested the World tongue-twister Champion.
I imagine he'll be given a tough sentence.

I bought a book titled 'How to scam people online' about three months ago... It still hasn't arrived.

People who write 'u' instead of 'you.' What do you do with all the time you save?

Sleep is my drug....my bed is my dealer and my alarm clock is the police.

Did you hear there is a coin shortage in America?
We're running out of common cents.

I won $3 million on the lottery this weekend so I decided to donate a quarter of it to charity.
Now I have $2,999,999.75.

Did you hear about the man who jumped off a bridge in France?
He was in Sein.

What did God say after creating man?
I must be able to do better than that.

I bought a dictionary and when I got home I realized all the pages were blank; I have no words for how angry I am.

I hate when I'm running on the treadmill for half an hour and look down to see it's been 4 minutes.

I ordered a chicken and an egg from Amazon.
I'll let you know.

So apparently RSVP'ing back to a wedding invite 'maybe next time' isn't the correct response.

Did you hear about these new reversible jackets?
I'm excited to see how they turn out.

The light at the end of the tunnel has been turned off due to budget cuts.

When I found out that my toaster wasn't waterproof, I was shocked.

A fine is a tax for doing wrong.
A tax is a fine for doing well.

When I lose the TV controller, it's always hidden in some remote destination.

Can't see an end. I have no control and I don't think there's an escape.

I don't even have a home anymore. Think it's time for a new keyboard.

I tried to escape the Apple store.
I couldn't because there were no Windows.

I'm the kind of guy who stops the microwave at 1 second just to feel like a bomb defuser.

Always borrow money from a pessimist.
He won't expect it back.

Top 3 situations that require witnesses: 1) Crimes 2) Accidents 3) Marriages.
Need I say more?

Engineers have successfully made a car that can run on parsley.
They are now attempting to make trains that can run on thyme...

What happens if you eat yeast and shoe polish?
Every morning you will rise and shine!

My friend claims that he 'accidentally' glued himself to his autobiography, but I don't believe him.
But that's his story, and he's sticking to it.

I hate when I am about to hug someone really sexy and my face hits the mirror.

I'd like to see things from your point of view but I can't seem to get my head that far up my ass.

My internet is so slow, it's just faster to drive to the Google headquarters and ask them shit in person.

My IQ test results just came in and I'm really relieved.
Thank God it's negative.

Retirement is wonderful. It's doing nothing without worrying about getting caught at it.

Living on earth may be expensive, but it includes an annual free trip around the sun.

You're so fake, Barbie is jealous.

I think it's wrong that only one company makes the game Monopoly.

Hey Christmas Tree, you got a lot of balls coming in here dressed like that.

I've been repeating the same mistakes in life for so long now,
I think I'll start calling them traditions.

Once upon a time there was a King who was only 12 inches tall.
He was a terrible King but he made a great ruler...

If you put your left shoe on the wrong foot... it's on the right foot.

When I see ads on TV with smiling, happy housewives using a new cleaning product, the only thing I want to buy are the meds they must be on.

When I was young, I was afraid of the dark.
Now when I get my electric bill, I am afraid of the light.

What does Jeff Bezos do every night before bed?
He puts his pajamazon.

They say "don't try this at home" so I'm coming over to your house to try it...

Everything becomes 100 times louder when you're trying not to wake someone up.

Facebook should have a limit on times you can update your relationship status.
After 3 it should default to 'unstable.'

My resolution was to read more so I put the subtitles on my tv.

I need a new bank account.
This one has run out of money.

If people could read my mind, I'd get punched in the face a lot.

We never really grow up, we only learn how to act in public.

I was hooked on auctions after only going once... going twice.

A mate said he saw several elderly men repairing shoes in the back of a van.
I reckon it's a load of old cobblers.

Dear Week, I'm so over you. I'm leaving you for your best friend, Weekend.
Don't try to find us for at least 2 days.

My neighbors are listening to great music.
Whether they like it or not.

I like when flies won't leave my car on long road trips.
Have fun moving to Kansas, you tiny idiot.

What's the difference between a guitar and a fish?
You can't tuna fish!

I went to buy a new mattress the other day.
I wasn't sure about it, so the salesman told me to go away and sleep on it.

Hippopotomonstrosesquippedaliophobia: Fear of long words.

What do you get when you cross a snowman and a vampire?
Frost bite.

I used to be a boy trapped in a woman's body.
But after 9 long months, I was finally born!

Sang the rainbow song in front of a police officer, got arrested for colourful language.

I bought a new Japanese car.
I turned on the radio... I don't understand a word they're saying.

Evening news is where they begin with "Good evening," and then proceed to tell you why it isn't.

What is the thinnest book in the world?
'What Men Know About Women.'

What did the blanket say when it fell off the bed?
"Oh sheet!"

Statistically 6 out of 7 Dwarfs are not Happy.

Sometimes, when I'm cruising the city in a $200K vehicle, I lean back and think, "If the bus driver doesn't speed up, I'll be late for work."

I have won first place in this Halloween costume contest 16 years in a row.
This year I am dressed as a hotdog. I'm on a roll.

What did the beach say as the tide came in?
"Long time no sea."

What do witches put on their hair?
Scare spray!

Why did the Easter egg hide?
Because he was a little chicken!

Which of Santa's reindeers needs to mind his manners the most?
'Rude'olph.

He's street smart.
Sesame Street smart.

Adult: Someone who has stopped growing at both ends and now grows in the middle.

I always wanted to learn to procrastinate... just never got around to it.

Tried watching The Neverending Story, couldn't finish it.

How do you make a blonde laugh on Saturday?
Tell her a joke on Wednesday!

16 Blondes are standing outside the bar. Why didn't they go in?
The sign said 18+.

People said I'd never get over my obsession with Phil Collins.
But take a look at me now.

I didn't realize how bad of a driver I was until my sat nav said, "In 400 feet, do a slight right, stop, and let me out."

Childhood is like being drunk; everyone remembers what you did, except you.

Why did the old woman fall into the well?
Because she couldn't see that well.

A woman's mind is cleaner than a man's: She changes it more often.

I put a new freezer next to the refrigerator, now they're just chilling.

Apparently I snore so loudly that it scares everyone in the car I'm driving.

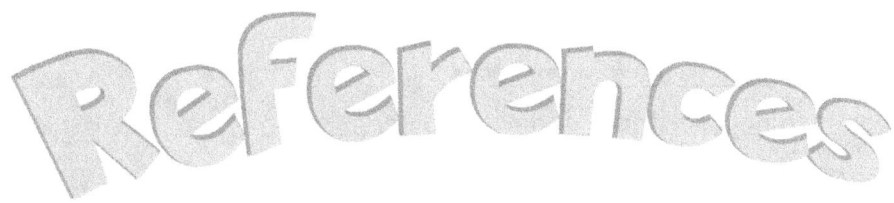

References

https://www.liveabout.com/funny-one-liners-4172815

https://jokesquotesfactory.com/funny-jokes-kids-children-family-friendly/

https://www.liveabout.com/nerd-jokes-4178877

https://www.liveabout.com/corny-dad-jokes-4137808

https://jokesquotesfactory.com/funny-sports-jokes/

https://www.countryliving.com/life/a27452412/best-dad-jokes/

https://www.boredpanda.com/funniest-two-line-jokes/

https://www.gq-magazine.co.uk/article/quick-fire-jokes-1

https://jokesquotesfactory.com/boss-jokes-work-funny-office/

https://jokesquotesfactory.com/love-jokes-cheeky-corny/

https://worstjokesever.com/

https://www.humorthatworks.com/database/funny-work-jokes-to-get-you-through-the-day/

https://jokesquotesfactory.com/funny-office-jokes-puns/

https://www.scotsman.com/read-this/100-of-the-funniest-short-jokes-that-will-have-you-laughing-in-seconds-47085

https://parade.com/1287449/marynliles/short-jokes/amp/

https://jokesquotesfactory.com/short-funny-jokes-one-liner/

https://jokesquotesfactory.com/jokes/office-jokes/

https://jokesquotesfactory.com/hilarious-marriage-jokes-husband-wife/

https://worstjokesever.com/party

https://funnyjokestoday.com/best-party-jokes/

https://onelinefun.com/

https://jokesquotesfactory.com/funny-finance-jokes/